Classic Fairy Tales
adapted by
Christine Deverell

©2002 Grandreams Books Limited.

Published by Grandreams Books Ltd,
4 North Parade, Bath, BA1 1LF, UK.

Grandreams Books Inc.,
360 Hurst Street, Linden, NJ 07036 USA

Printed in China.

· C O N T E N T S ·

Snow White and the Seven Dwarfs   4

Jack and the Beanstalk   14

Puss in Boots   26

Goldilocks and the Three Bears   38

Sleeping Beauty   48

Little Red Riding Hood   59

Rumpelstiltskin   71

The Frog Prince   80

Snow White and the Seven Dwarfs

ILLUSTRATED BY DAVID LONG

It was the middle of winter. A Queen sat by a window made of the finest black ebony. As she looked out at the snow, she pricked her finger and three drops of blood fell onto it.

She gazed at the red drops in the white snow and said, "I wish my little daughter to be as white as the snow, as red as blood and as black as ebony ."

And her daughter was beautiful, with skin as white as snow, cheeks as rosy as the blood, and hair as black as ebony. Her name was Snow White.

Sadly the Queen died, and Snow White's father married another wife. This Queen had a magic mirror. She would gaze at herself and say,

"Mirror, mirror, on the wall, Who is the fairest of them all?"

And the mirror would reply,

"You, O Queen, are the fairest in the land."

But one day, when she looked into the mirror, it answered her,

"You my Queen, may lovely be
But Snow White is by far the most beautiful in the land."

The Queen called one of her servants and ordered him to take Snow White out into the woods. "I never want to see her again", she screeched! The servant was very unhappy and did not want to hurt Snow White. So he left her in the wood, and returned to the Queen to tell her that Snow White was dead.

Poor Snow White was alone and afraid as she wandered in the wood. As night fell, she reached a cottage.

It was the home of seven dwarfs. Inside, she found a table neatly laid with seven small loaves of bread and seven little glasses of wine. Against the wall were seven small beds.

Snow White was very hungry, so she helped herself to a little bread from each loaf, and a sip of wine from each glass.

Then she lay down and fell asleep.

When they returned from their day's work, the seven dwarfs were not at all pleased with the mess that they saw on the table.

They turned around and found Snow White sleeping soundly.

At first they grumbled and complained to one another, but then, they all gazed in amazement at her beauty, and agreed to let her sleep until morning.

Snow White stayed with the dwarfs. While they were hard at work in the Diamond Mine, she looked after their cottage and prepared the meals every day. One day, the Queen looked into her mirror and asked her usual question.

The mirror replied;

"You are the fairest in this place.

But by far the most beautiful face

Belongs to Snow White."

The Queen was furious. "I thought she was dead!" she cried. She disguised herself as an old gypsy woman and went

off into the woods in search of Snow White. She carried with her a basket of apples. One of the apples was poisoned on one side. When she came upon the cottage, she knocked on the door.

Snow White opened the window, looked out and said,

"I dare not let anyone in."

"Never mind dear. Just let me give you one of my beautiful apples." Snow White did not want to take it, but the Queen said, "Look, I will take a bite and you will see that it is safe."

Snow White then took a bite of the apple and fell down dead. When the dwarfs returned from work that day they were very unhappy to find Snow White lying lifeless on the ground. She was so beautiful and they wanted to look at her forever, so they laid her in a glass coffin.

Snow White looked as if she were only sleeping. One day a prince rode by and begged the dwarfs to let him take Snow White away with him. They refused at first, but then they took pity on him, and granted his wish. As soon as he lifted the coffin, a piece of apple fell from Snow White's lips, and she awoke.

The Prince asked Snow White to
go with him to his father's palace
and marry him.

The wicked Queen was invited
to the marriage feast, and when she
arrived and saw that Snow White
was the bride, she choked with rage,
fell ill and died. But Snow White
and the Prince reigned happily over
that land for many, many years.

13

Jack and the Beanstalk

ILLUSTRATED BY IVANA SVABIC CANNON

14

There was once a poor widow who had an only son called Jack. He was so lazy he never did any work, and as time went by, they became poorer and poorer.

One fine summer's day Jack's mother decided to send him to the market to sell their cow. It was all they had left in the world and even she no longer gave them milk.

Jack had not gone very far when he met an old man.

"Where are you going with that cow, young man?" said he.

"I am going to the market to sell her," Jack replied.

"Well, this is your lucky day," said the old man, "for I will gladly take her off your hands in exchange for these five magic beans. If you plant them, they will grow as high as the sky by tomorrow morning."

Jack thought this was a fair exchange, as it meant he could go home right away and spend the rest of the day lazing in the sun.

"Look mother," he cried as he ran into the house, "I have sold our cow for these amazing beans!"

"You are stupid as well as lazy," she said as she snatched the beans from his hand and threw them out of the window. Then she sent him to bed without any supper.

Jack slept until late the next morning and when he woke he was not sure where he was. His room was dark, and when

he opened the curtains he saw huge leaves and red flowers covering his window. He dressed himself quickly and ran downstairs and into the garden.

Jack could not believe what he saw. Just outside the window where his mother had thrown the magic beans there grew a mighty beanstalk, reaching towards the sky, so that the top of it was hidden in the clouds. Without wasting a second Jack began to climb.

He climbed higher than the tree tops, higher than the clouds until he reached the blue sky and stepped out onto a long, straight, white road. Jack was very hungry by this time, so he followed the road, hoping to find a place where he could beg for some breakfast.

To his delight, he came to a castle, with a very large woman standing at the door. "Good morning," he said politely, "would you be so kind as to give me some breakfast?"

"I think you had better run away as fast as you can," said the woman, "unless you want to become a breakfast yourself. My husband is an Ogre who loves nothing better than fried little boys on toast for his breakfast."

Jack was too hungry to run back along the road, so he pleaded with the woman to give him something to eat. "You can hide me from your husband when he comes," said Jack.

Now the Ogre's wife was a kind woman, and she took Jack in and gave him some bread and milk. He had only just finished eating when, thump, thump, thump, he heard the Ogre walking down the road. The woman grabbed Jack and hid him in the oven.

The Ogre came into the kitchen and roared at the top of his voice: "Fee-fi-fo-fum, I smell the blood of an Englishman. Be he alive, or be he dead, I'll grind his bones to make my

18

bread." "Nonsense!" said the wife, "you are always saying you can smell Englishmen. Now sit down and have your breakfast."

Jack peeped out of his hiding place and was terrified to see what a huge, ugly monster he was. The table was piled high with food and the Ogre ate all of it.

Then he called to his wife, "Bring me my bags of gold!" She cleared the table and put the gold in front of him. There he sat counting and counting the coins until his eyelids began to droop and his head nodded slowly down and rested on the table; he fell fast asleep, snoring so loudly that people on the earth below thought they heard a thunderstorm.

When Jack peeped out and saw all that gold he knew this was his big chance. He crept out of the oven, and as he passed the sleeping Ogre Jack reached up and grabbed one of the bags of gold. He ran away from the castle and down the straight, white road as fast as his legs would carry him, back to the top of the beanstalk. He climbed down through the green leaves until he reached his own little garden again.

"Mother, look what I have brought you from the top of the beanstalk!" Jack cried as he emptied the bag of gold coins onto the kitchen table.

The poor widow was pleased to have her son home again, and now they had money to buy all they needed.

One day, Jack took out the bag and saw that there was not much gold left, so he decided to climb the beanstalk again. He disguised himself so that the woman would not recognise him, and once again she let him in and gave him some food.

The Ogre returned to the castle in the evening and Jack hid in a huge copper pot. Then he called to his wife to bring him his golden hen. The wife brought the hen and placed it on the table.

"Lay!" roared the Ogre, and the hen laid an egg of solid gold.

"Lay another!" and the hen laid an even larger golden egg. When Jack saw the golden eggs his eyes popped out of his head.

Soon, the Ogre fell asleep at the table and when Jack was sure that no one else was about, he climbed out of the copper pot and grabbed the Ogre's hen.

The hen started to squawk as Jack ran towards the door, and the Ogre woke up.

A few seconds passed before he realised that the hen was not on the table, and when he looked out of the window, he saw Jack with his prize bird under his arm, running for all he was worth along the straight white road. The Ogre chased

after Jack with huge
strides. The people in the
world below thought that
they could hear an earthquake.
Even though Jack was running
faster than he had ever run in
his life, the Ogre was almost
upon him when Jack reached
the beanstalk.

Just as the Ogre
reached out his hand to
grab Jack and
retrieve his
precious
hen, Jack
slipped
nimbly
down the
beanstalk.
The Ogre
paused for a few

moments, wondering if this strange plant would carry his weight. Then he began to climb slowly down after Jack. The beanstalk began to sway and creak, and Jack, realising the Ogre was following, went even faster. When Jack reached his garden he called out,

"Quick! Quick! Get me an axe, mother!" He seized the axe, handed her the golden hen, and began to chop at the mighty beanstalk. It swayed and creaked and then it fell with a tremendous crash!

The Ogre lay dead under the leaves. Jack and his mother lived happily all their lives with the golden hen, that brought them more riches than they knew how to spend.

Puss in Boots

ILLUSTRATED BY JAN NESBITT

Once upon a time there lived a poor miller who had three sons. When he died, all he owned was divided between his sons; the eldest had the mill, the second son had the donkey and cart, and all that was left for the youngest son was the miller's black cat.

The boy was very fond of the cat, but could not see how she would ever make his fortune.

As he stroked her gently, she said, "Don't worry, master. If you do what I tell you, you will see what I can do for you. First, get me a large bag and a pair of boots." The miller's son took the last few shillings he had, and bought the cat a large bag and a pair of yellow boots.

The cat put on her new boots and went out into the garden. She picked some lettuce and put it in the new bag. Then off she went across the fields until she found a rabbit hole. She put the bag down with its mouth wide open so the lettuce could be seen. Then she hid herself behind a low hedge.

Soon, a fat grey rabbit popped his head out of the hole. He smelt the fresh lettuce and jumped into the bag to eat it.

Puss-in-Boots immediately leapt from behind the hedge and swiftly drew the strings of the bag together and the fat rabbit was caught.

Then Puss slung the bag over her shoulder and set off in her yellow boots until she came to the King's palace. She presented herself to the King, and bowing low said, "Your Majesty, I have brought you a fat rabbit from the estate of my master, the Marquis of Carabas." The King was amused at the sight of a black cat in yellow boots, but he graciously accepted the gift.

The next day Puss put a handful of grain into her bag and

went out to the fields. She
set the bag as before and lay
down beside it pretending to
be dead.

This time two pheasants
came and started to eat the
grain. She waited for the
right moment, and quickly
gathered up the strings of the bag, catching both birds inside.
Once more she set off for the palace, and presented herself to
the King.

"My master, the Marquis of Carabas, begs your acceptance
of these two pheasants," said Puss-in Boots, bowing gracefully.

"Tell your master," said the King, "that I am pleased to accept his gift. He must have a very fine estate."

"Oh indeed, it is, very fine," said Puss as she bowed and took her leave of the King.

As she passed through the great halls, she heard that the King and his daughter were going to drive beside the river that afternoon. Puss raced home to her master, and told him about her visit to the palace, and then commanded him,

"I want you to go and swim in the river and if anyone

asks your name, you are to say that you are the Marquis of Carabas."

So he left Puss-in-Boots to guard his clothes and went and swam in the river.

Puss carefully hid the clothes under a pile of stones, and waited for the royal carriage. As it approached, Puss ran out, shouting, "Help! Help! The Marquis of Carabas is drowning!"

The King ordered the coach to stop and sent his servants to rescue the Marquis. Then Puss went up to the carriage, and with his hat in his hand, bowed to the King and Princess and said, "We are indeed so grateful that you happened to be passing just now. But, alas, a thief has stolen my master's clothes."

The King sent a servant to the palace to get a suit, and when the miller's son put it on, he looked just like a prince.

"This is my master, the Marquis of Carabas," said Puss to the King and Princess as she graciously introduced him.

"We hope you will drive on and dine with the Marquis."

"It will be a pleasure," replied the King, and he invited the Marquis to ride in his carriage.

Puss ran ahead of the carriage and took a short cut across the fields. Back on the road, she came across some haymakers.

They stared at the sight of a black cat in yellow boots, and she told them sternly,

"When the King passes this way and asks to whom this field of hay belongs, you are to say,

'To the Marquis of Carabas, your Majesty.'

If you don't, you will be chopped into little pieces."

Then she ran on until she came to a field where reapers were busy cutting the wheat.

"When the King passes this way," said Puss, "and asks to whom this field of wheat belongs, you are to say,

'To the Marquis of Carabas, your Majesty.'

If you don't, you will chopped into little pieces."

Now the land really belonged to a terrible Ogre, and Puss-in-Boots carried on running until she reached his great castle.

No one ever visited him because he was so frightening, but when he opened the door, Puss walked straight in, showing off her fine boots.

33

The Ogre was so shocked that he could only stare at her.

"I have heard that you can turn yourself into a wild beast; is that true?" said Puss, calmly. "Well naturally." said the Ogre swelling with pride, and then in a flash he became a roaring lion.

Poor Puss ran and hid herself up the chimney! The Ogre changed himself back again and laughed at Puss, who said,

"It is truly wonderful that an Ogre such as yourself can become a great lion, but I very much doubt that you could change into a tiny creature, say, a mouse?"

"Pooh! no problem at all," said the Ogre, and in an instant he had disappeared and Puss saw a tiny mouse running across the room.

She pounced and seized the creature, and with one shake, the Ogre was dead.

At this moment, the King's carriage drew up outside the castle.

"You have a splendid estate," said the King to the miller's son, for sure enough, the haymakers and reapers had obeyed Puss, and told him the land belonged to the Marquis of Carabas;

"And this is a magnificent castle."

They went inside and sat down to a feast.

"This young man would make a good husband for my daughter," thought the King. "Your title does not match your wealth. I shall make you a Prince." The Princess loved the Prince, and he loved her.

So they were married, and lived together happily in the Ogre's castle. Puss-in Boots lived in comfort to the end of her life and she never had to hunt again.

Goldilocks and the Three Bears

ILLUSTRATED BY RICHARD DEVERELL

There were once upon a time three bears who lived in a house in the woods. There was a Little Baby Bear, a Mother Bear and a Big Father Bear.

Each had a bowl for its porridge: a tiny bowl for the

Little Baby Bear, a medium sized bowl for Mother Bear, and a great big bowl for the Big Father Bear.

Each had a chair to sit on: a tiny chair for the Little Baby Bear, a medium sized chair for Mother Bear and a great big chair for the Big Father Bear.

Each had a bed to sleep in: a tiny bed for the Little Baby Bear, a medium sized bed for Mother Bear and a great big bed for the Big Father Bear.

One day, after they had made the porridge for their breakfast, they decided to go for a walk to give the porridge time to cool down. While they were out, a little girl named Goldilocks passed the house.

She was not a good, polite little girl, and she peered through the windows and peeped

through the keyhole. When she saw that no one was at home, she lifted the latch and went inside.

She saw the bowls of porridge on the breakfast table and not having eaten yet, decided to help herself. She tried the Big Father Bear's porridge, but that was too salty. Then she tried the Mother Bear's porridge, and that was too sweet.

Then she tried the Little Baby Bear's porridge, and that was just right; neither too salty, nor too sweet, and she ate it all up.

Then Goldilocks sat down

in Big Father Bear's chair. It was much too hard, so she tried Mother Bear's chair. That was much too soft. So she tried Little Baby Bear's chair, and it felt perfect. But after she had sat in Little Baby Bear's chair for just a few seconds, the leg broke, and Goldilocks crashed to the floor!

Goldilocks went upstairs, hoping to find a comfortable bed. She lay down on Big Father Bear's bed. It was much too hard, so she tried Mother Bear's bed. That was much too soft.

So she tried Little Baby Bear's bed, and it felt perfect. She got right under the covers and fell fast asleep.

While she slept, the three bears came home for their breakfast. Goldilocks had made quite a mess on the table.

"Who's been eating my porridge?" boomed Big Father Bear in his great, gruff voice. "Who's been eating my porridge?" said Mother Bear in her cross voice. "And who's been eating my porridge?" cried Little Baby Bear in his squeaky little voice, "And they've eaten it all up!"

They looked around the room and saw that the furniture had been moved. They went over to their chairs. "Who's been sitting on my chair?" boomed Big Father Bear in his great, gruff voice. For Goldilocks had used the hard cushion to wipe the porridge off her fingers. "Who's been sitting on my chair?" said Mother Bear in her cross voice. For Goldilocks had left a big dent in the soft cushion. "And who's been sitting on my chair?" cried Little Baby Bear in his squeaky little voice, "And they've broken it!" By now poor Little Baby Bear was in tears.

Together the three bears went upstairs to the bedroom. First, they came to Big Father Bear's bed. "Who's been lying on my bed?" boomed Big Father Bear in his great, gruff voice. For Goldilocks had crumpled the sheets. "Who's been lying on my bed?" said Mother Bear in her cross voice. For Goldilocks had thrown the soft pillows onto the floor, and left a dirty mark on the fine quilt.

"And who is that sleeping in my bed?" cried Little Baby Bear in his squeaky little voice through his tears. "Look! She ate my porridge! She broke my chair! She made a mess in our house! And now, there she is! She's sleeping in my bed!"

Suddenly, Goldilocks woke up and saw the three

46

bears staring down at her crossly. She sprung out of the bed and sped down the stairs, out of the front door and into the wood. The three bears heard Goldilocks crying out: "There's bears in the wood! Help! Help! There's bears in the wood!" Her voice faded into silence, and the three bears were never bothered by her again.

Sleeping Beauty

ILLUSTRATED BY JAN NESBITT

A long time ago there lived a King and Queen who were very sad, because they had no children. One day, as the Queen sat by a pond in the castle gardens thinking of her wishes, a frog hopped on to a lily pad in front of her and said, "Your wish will be granted. Before a year has passed, you shall have a daughter."

Everything happened as the frog had said. A little girl was born, and the King was so happy that he ordered a great celebration feast to be held.

All their friends and relatives, and Kings and Queens from other kingdoms were invited, together with twelve fairies who would bring special gifts to the Princess.

Now it happened that there were thirteen such fairies living in this domain, and everyone knows that thirteen is an unlucky number. So one of these was not invited to the feast, and she was not a happy fairy.

The day for the feast arrived and all the guests were gathered in the Great Hall of the King's castle. Every guest brought a gift, and the twelve fairies lined up to bestow their special gifts on the baby.

"I give her virtue," said one. "I give her beauty," said another. Yet another gave her riches, another health and so on, until she had all the gifts that any mother or father could wish their child to own.

Eleven fairies gave their gifts, and as the twelfth stepped forward, the door flew open, and in marched the thirteenth who was determined to have her revenge.

"On her fifteenth birthday the Princess shall prick her finger on a needle and die!" she exclaimed loudly, and turned her back on the whole company and left. Then the twelfth fairy, who had not yet given her gift, stepped forward. She said that she could not undo the wicked fairy's curse, but she could soften it.

"The King's daughter will not die, but will sleep for a hundred years."

But the King and Queen hoped to save their daughter from this fate, and ordered that all the needles in the Kingdom

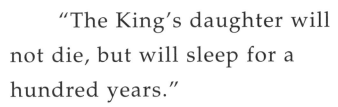

should be destroyed.

The Princess grew to be beautiful, wise, friendly and well behaved. Everyone who knew her, loved her.

Now it happened

that on the morning of the day of her fifteenth birthday, the King and Queen were not at home, so the Princess was alone in the castle.

She wandered around from room to room, along the corridors and up and down the splendid staircases until she came upon an old tower. She climbed the narrow, winding stairs until she reached a door, in the lock of which was a rusty key. The Princess turned the key, the door sprang open, and there in the room she saw an old woman with a spinning wheel.

"Good morning, my good lady," said the Princess,

"what are you doing here?" "I am spinning," she replied, "here, you can try it."

No sooner had she taken hold of the spindle, the Princess pricked her finger and fell back onto a bed in a deep sleep. Everyone in the castle fell asleep; The King and Queen who

had just returned home, their courtiers and servants. The horses in the stable, the doves on the roof, the flies on the walls, and even the fire in the hearth all appeared to die in the same moment.

A thick bramble hedge quickly grew around the castle until not even the flag on the high tower could be seen. The story was told throughout many lands of the beautiful Princess asleep in a lost castle where every living creature lay motionless.

Many princes came and tried to cut their way through the thorns to reach her, but they were unsuccessful. After many years had passed, another King's son came by and heard the story of the sleeping Princess. He was not to be daunted by the failure of those who had gone before him.

It happened that one hundred years had very nearly passed since the great sleep had fallen on the castle. As this young Prince approached the thick, bramble hedge, the thorns turned into fine flowers and parted to let him through.

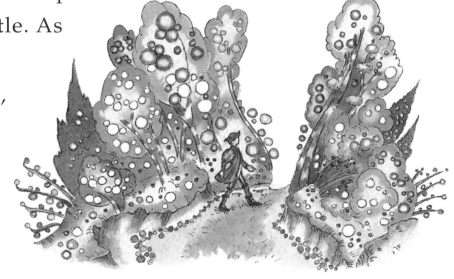

In the courtyard he saw the horses and dogs lying fast asleep.

He stepped over the bodies of the courtiers in the Great Hall and saw the King and Queen asleep on their thrones.

The Prince looked in all the rooms in the castle, and at last he came to the tower and opened the door of the little chamber where the Princess slept. She looked so beautiful that

the Prince could not help but gaze upon her, and he bent down and kissed her. Just as he did so, she opened her eyes and smiled at him.

Then the King and Queen awoke, and the whole court, the servants, the horses, the dogs and the flies on the wall. The fire in the hearth began to burn brightly. The whole castle was once more alive with the sound of happy voices as if nothing had happened, for the hundred years sleep had made no difference to anyone.

Very soon, the wedding of The Prince and his Sleeping
Beauty was celebrated with great splendour, and they lived
together happy and contented to the end of their lives.

Little Red Riding Hood

ILLUSTRATED BY DAVID LONG

A very long time ago, so many wild beasts prowled about in the forests that no one was ever surprised to meet a wolf or a bear. A little girl, whom everyone called Red Riding Hood, lived in a cottage on the edge of a

wood with her mother and father, who worked as a woodcutter. Red Riding Hood was not her real name, but it was given her because she always wore a red hooded coat that her grandmother had made for her.

Now this grandmother lived alone in a rose covered cottage on the other side of the wood, and Red Riding Hood loved to visit her. One day little girl's mother called her and said, "Why don't you go to your grandmother's house for tea today? She has not been well, so I have baked her a cake and

made her some lemonade." Handing her the gifts in a basket she added, "Do not stray from the path and do not stop to talk to anyone on the way." Red Riding Hood promised to go straight to the cottage; so her mother tied on her red hood, kissed her goodbye, and off she went.

She had not gone very far along the path when she met a wolf. "Good morning, Little Red Riding Hood, where are you

going today?" he asked her. "Good morning Mr Wolf" she said, politely, "I am going to visit my grandmother." "And what are you carrying in the basket?" asked the wolf.

"Cake and lemonade for our tea," Little Red Riding Hood replied. "So where does your grandmother live?" asked the wolf in his sweetest voice. "I continue along this path, take the left path when it divides in two, and walk for another ten minutes.It's the cottage that is covered with roses."

"Aha, your grandmother likes flowers, does she? Why don't you pick some of these from beside the path and take them to her?" suggested the wolf.

Then the wolf trotted off, and Little Red Riding Hood thought it would be a great idea to gather a posy for her grandmother. First, she picked a few flowers from beside the path, but then she saw that there were some prettier ones under the trees. So she disobeyed her mother's command, and stepped off the path.

The sun was shining through the branches and birds were singing happily. Little Red Riding Hood suddenly remembered that she should have kept to the path and gone straight to her grandmother's cottage, so she picked up her basket and the bunch of flowers, and set off once again.

Meanwhile, the wolf had raced ahead, following Little Red Riding Hood's directions to the cottage.

"The rose covered cottage, she said, so this must be it.

Aha!"he said to himself, "Now I shall gobble up the old grandmother, and I'll have Little Red Riding Hood for

dessert." He knocked on the door very gently.

"Lift the latch and come in." said the old lady.

The wolf lifted the latch and burst through the door, and gobbled up the poor old

grandmother in one mouthful. Then he found one of her big frilly nightcaps in a drawer, pulled it over his ears and jumped into bed, taking care to draw the sheet well up under his chin.

A few moments later Red Riding Hood tapped on the door of the cottage.

"Lift the latch and come in," said the wolf in his softest voice. But this voice did not sound like Little Red Riding Hood's grandmother, and the little girl wondered what was wrong.

"Mother has sent some cake and lemonade for our tea, but grandmother, how strange your voice sounds, and why are you in bed?"

"I have a cold on my chest," answered the wolf.

"Come here, my dear and sit on the bed."

As Red Riding Hood approached the bed, she could not believe what she saw.

"Oh Grandmother, what big eyes you have!" she said.

"All the better to see you with my dear," answered the wolf.

"But Grandmother, what big ears you have."

"All the better to hear you with, my dear."

"But Grandmother, what big teeth you have."

"All the better to gobble you up with my dear," said the wolf as he leapt out of the bed.

Little Red Riding Hood turned and ran screaming towards the door.

The wolf had just caught her red cloak in his mouth when the door burst open, and Little Red Riding Hood's own father came rushing in.

With one blow of his axe he struck the wicked wolf

dead, and picked up Little Red Riding Hood in his arms and hugged her. "Oh Father, I think the wolf must have eaten up dear Grandmother," sobbed Little Red Riding Hood.

So he took out his knife, and carefully cut the wolf open. Inside, they found the old Grandmother safe and sound, for the wolf in his greed had swallowed her whole, and his teeth had not touched her.

They all sat down to enjoy their cake and lemonade, and
Little Red Riding Hood promised that she would never talk to
any wolf that she might meet in the woods, and she would
always obey her mother and never stray from the path.

Rumpelstiltskin

ILLUSTRATED BY STEPHEN ANGEL

Once there was a poor miller who had a very beautiful daughter. He was so poor, he couldn't pay his taxes, and when the King threatened to put him in prison, the miller in desperation said, "I have a daughter who can spin gold out of straw."

"Then bring her to me immediately," ordered the King. The frightened girl was led to a room which was filled with a huge pile of straw.

"Spin all this into gold before morning, or you will be punished." She pleaded to be excused, for she knew that she was not able to spin gold out of straw, but it was no use. The door was locked and she sat there alone and wept.

After a while, the door opened and in walked a little man. "Why are you sad?" he asked.

"The King has ordered me to spin all this straw into gold, and I don't know how to do it." little man.

The girl gave him her necklace, and he sat down to work, spinning the straw into fine gold.

By morning he was finished. The King was delighted with what he saw, but he wanted more. So he took the miller's daughter to a larger room filled with straw and told her to spin it into gold by the next morning. Again she sat down and wept.

Soon, the little man came into the room and said,

"What will you give me if I do this for you?" She gave him her gold ring, and he worked until morning, when the task was complete.

The King was greedy and wanted even more gold, so the next evening he took the girl to an even larger room, filled to the rafters with straw. He said, "If you can do this tonight, you will be my wife."

The little man came in as before and asked her,

"What will you give me to spin all this into gold for you?"

She despaired, for she had nothing left to give him.

"Then promise me," said the little man, "your first child when you are queen."

The miller's daughter could only agree to give the little man what he wanted though she hoped that she would never have to keep her promise. The little man spun a huge pile of gold, and not a piece of straw was left. In the morning the King found all he wanted, and the miller's daughter became his Queen.

A year passed, and the Queen gave birth to a lovely daughter. She was so happy that she forgot about the funny little man and the promise she made. Until one day he appeared and reminded her of it.

She offered him all the treasure of the kingdom but he refused to accept it. She cried and cried because she could not bear to part with her little baby.

The little man gave in to her pleading saying,

"Very well, I will give you three days, and if in that time you can guess my name, then you may keep your child."

The Queen stayed up all night thinking of all the names she had ever heard and writing them down in a long list.

The next day, the little man came to her room and she began to work through the list. Peter, John, Mark, Isaac, Thomas, Henry, Jeremiah . . . But with every name she tried she received the same reply:

"No! That's not my name."

On the second day she tried all the strangest names that she had heard of, and some that she made up herself, like Roofabeef, Gug and Boogie. But the little man just laughed and said,

"You will never guess my name!"

The Queen sent her servants out to see if they could discover any other names.

77

All but one returned with no new names for her. But late in the evening, as the remaining servant was making his way back to the castle, he heard a little man singing in the woods:

"Merrily the feast I'll make,

Today I'll brew, tomorrow bake;

Merrily I'll dance and sing,

For next day a stranger bring:

Little does my lady dream

Rumpelstiltskin is my name!"

This faithful servant told the Queen of his fortunate discovery, and when on the third day her little visitor arrived, she asked him, "Is your name William? "No."

"Is it Charles?" "No."

"Could it be . . . Rumpelstiltskin?"

"Who told you that? Who told you that?" cried the little man; and he shook his fists and stamped his feet so hard that he made a hole in the floor and fell right into it.

Moaning and groaning, he pulled himself out of the hole and ran away. The Queen lived happily with the King and her daughter, and they were never bothered by Rumpelstiltskin again.

The Frog Prince

ILLUSTRATED BY IVANA SVABIC CANNON

80

Long ago there lived a king with several beautiful daughters. But the youngest was so beautiful that even the Sun himself was enchanted when she came out to play in the sunshine. She would often go out into the garden by herself, and one afternoon she was dancing around on the grass, throwing a golden ball up into the air and catching it again.

The ball glinted in the sunshine and the Princess missed catching it when for a moment the bright light blinded her eyes.

She laughed as she ran down the slope chasing after it. Then she threw the golden ball high into the air and watched

in horror as it fell into a well so deep that it seemed to take forever before she heard a feint plop as it hit the water at the bottom.

The Princess sat down beside the well and wept. She cried louder and louder until she heard a voice call out,

"Why are you crying O King's daughter? Your tears would melt even a stone to pity."

She looked around to the spot where the voice was coming from and saw a Frog's ugly face staring at her.

"Was it you that spoke? I am weeping for my golden ball which has fallen into this well and I don't know how I will ever get it back."

"Never mind," said the Frog, "I can get it back

for you. But what will you give me if I do?"

"What would you like, dear Frog? You can have my jewels, my pearls or my golden crown."

"I have no use for these things," replied the Frog,

"but if you will love me, and let me play with you, sit at your table, eat from your plate, drink from your cup, and sleep in your bed, then I will climb into the well and retrieve your golden ball."

"Oh, I will promise you all these things, if only I can have my ball," she cried, thinking that she would never have to keep a promise she made to a Frog. But the Frog dropped into the well, picked up the golden ball in his mouth and climbed all the way out. The Princess thanked him, took the ball and ran off, as fast as she could, back to the palace.

"Stop! Stop! Wait for me! I cannot keep up with you," croaked the Frog in his loudest voice, but she did not even hear him.

The Princess soon forgot the Frog and the promise she had made, and the frog hopped back into the lake near the well. One day, the King's daughter was sitting at table with her father and his courtiers when she heard a knock at the door. She went to open it and there before her stood the Frog. The Princess turned very pale and quickly shut the door. As she sat

down to eat again her
father asked her if there
was a giant at the door to
frighten her so.

"No father, it is not
a giant, but an ugly
Frog."

"And what does
the Frog want?" said
the King.

The Princess told
her father the story of
how she lost her golden ball in the well and the promise she
made to the Frog. Then the King said,

"A promise made must be kept.

Go and let him in." So reluctantly she went and opened
the door and the Frog followed her back to her place.

"Pick me up," he said, and the King ordered her to obey.
She placed the Frog on her chair, and immediately he sprang
up onto the table and demanded,

"Move your plate close to me and we will eat together."

Everyone at the table could see she was very unwilling,
but she did what she had promised. The Frog relished every
mouthful but the King's daughter felt sick and could not eat

any more of her food. When she got down from the table she lifted the Frog onto the floor and he followed her out into the garden to play. The little Frog went everywhere with her and when she thought she could escape from him, she ran as fast as she

could back to the palace.

Remembering her promise that she would let the Frog sleep in her bed, she ran straight upstairs to her bedroom and bolted the door. Just as the Princess got into bed, she heard a feint knocking sound.

"Who's there?" she called, her voice trembling.

"Please let me in; you promised I could sleep in your bed, and your father said a promise made must be kept."

The Princess opened the door and the Frog hopped across the room

and clambered up onto the bed. The frightened girl curled up as far away from the Frog as she could, but was unable to sleep all night.

The next day, the little Frog refused to leave the Princess's side. He played with her, sat on her lap when she rode with her father in his carriage and ate from her plate at meal times.

The poor girl was growing tired of this ugly little creature and feared she might never be rid of him.

"Will you never go away and leave me alone, you ugly little Frog?" she asked him tearfully.

"First, you must kiss me, and then if you really want me to leave you sweet Princess, I will go."

Kiss a Frog? The poor girl thought she would rather die. But so desperate was she to be free of him that she took a deep breath, closed her eyes, and offered him her lips to kiss.

When she opened her eyes she found that the Frog had indeed disappeared, and in his place stood a tall, handsome young Prince.

He told her how a wicked witch had transformed him and that only she could set him free from the spell. She fell in love with him instantly and they ran back to the palace to find her father. He gave his consent to their marriage and the Prince and Princess lived very happily in his kingdom for many years.